A Note to Parents

For many children, learning math is difficult and "I hate math!" is their first response — to which many parents silently add "Me, too!" Children often see adults comfortably reading and writing, but they rarely have such models for mathematics. And math fear can be catching!

The easy-to-read stories in this **Hello Math Reader!** series were written to give children a positive introduction to mathematics and parents a pleasurable reacquaintance with a subject that is important in everyone's life. **Hello Math Reader!** stories make mathematical ideas accessible, interesting, and fun for children. The activities and suggestions at the end of each book provide parents with a hands-on approach to help children develop mathematical interest and confidence.

Enjoy the mathematics!

• Give your child a chance to retell the story. The more familiar children are with the story, the more they will understand its mathematical concepts.

• Use the colorful illustrations to help children "hear and see" the math at work in the story.

• Treat the math activities as games to be played for fun. Follow your child's lead. Spend time on those activities that engage your child's interest and curiosity.

• Activities, especially ones using physical materials, help make abstract mathematical ideas concrete.

Learning is a messy process and learning about math calls for children to become immersed in lively experiences that help them make sense of mathematical concepts and symbols.

Although learning about numbers is basic to math, other ideas, such as identifying shapes and patterns, measuring, collecting and interpreting data, reasoning logically, and thinking about chance are also important. By reading these stories and having fun with the activities, you will help your child enthusiastically say "**Hello, math**," instead of "I hate math."

—Marilyn Burns
National Mathematics Educator
Author of *The I Hate Mathematics! Book*

To Dan and Patty, for all their patient proofreading.
— D.R.

ISBN 0-439-24231-2

12 11 10 9 8 7 6 5 4 3 2 1   2 3 4 5 6 7/0

Printed in the U.S.A.   24
First Scholastic printing, September 2002

Recess Countdown

written and illustrated by Dana Regan

Hello Math Reader! — Level 3

SCHOLASTIC INC.
New York   Toronto   London   Auckland   Sydney
Mexico City   New Delhi   Hong Kong   Buenos Aires

Rrring! The noontime bell rings.

"Recess!" Kim calls.

"Yes!" cheers Carlos.

Kim gulps down the rest of her milk and tosses the carton into the trash. Carlos races to return his lunch tray. "Last one outside is a rotten egg!" he calls.

"Slow down," their teacher, Ms. Jensen, says. "Let's line up for recess."

Kim, Carlos, and their 20 classmates form two lines. Eleven pairs of kids walk quickly to the door to the playground.

"Let's play kickball!" suggests Kim.

"Good choice!" says Carlos.

Carlos and Kim are picked for the same team. The two kickball teams start to play. After a few rounds, the score is tied at 16–16. The bases are loaded. Kim is up.

"Kick it hard, Kim!" shouts Carlos from second base.

$$16 + 1 + 1 + 1 + 1 = 20$$

The other team's captain sends the ball rolling toward Kim. Kim pulls back her leg and kicks—hard! She kicks the ball so hard, it sails over everyone's head! Kim races toward first base. All the players on the other bases start running, too. One run scores, then another, then another. Then Kim rounds third base. She keeps running.

"Home run!" shouts Kim as she crosses home plate.

"We win, twenty to sixteen!" Carlos cheers.

Kim, Carlos, and the rest of the team give each other high fives. Then Kim says, "Let's play something else."

"How about dodgeball?" asks Carlos.

If two's company and three's a crowd, what's four and five?

Nine.

This time, Carlos and Kim are on opposite teams. Each team starts with 26 players. By the end of the first round, Carlos gets out seven players. By the end of the second round, he's tagged out 12 players.

"You're good at this game, Carlos!" Kim says. "You've already subtracted nineteen players from our team, including me! Since I'm out, I'm going to see what Nina and the girls are doing."

7 + 12 = 19
26 − 19 = 7

"What's up?" asks Kim as she joins some girls in the corner of the playground.

"We're having a jumping contest," answers Nina. "We want to see who can jump the most times without making a mistake. Do you want to try, Kim? Grace is first, then Lisa, then Kate, then me, and then you can go. We'll all count."

Grace jumps 43 times. Lisa jumps 37 times. Kate jumps 54 times. Nina jumps 39 times. Kim jumps 51 times.

"You win!" Kim tells Kate.

Everybody congratulates Kate. Meanwhile, Kim hears some first graders nearby arguing about the tire swing.

Kim walks over to the tire swing. One little girl is swinging. Six other first graders are watching. They look unhappy.

"What's the matter?" asks Kim.

"She's hogging the swing!" whines a boy with two missing front teeth. "We want a turn."

"I have an idea," says Kim. "I'll time you with my watch. Everyone can swing for the same amount of time. There are fourteen minutes left in recess and there are seven of you. If you each take a two-minute ride, everyone will get a turn. Fair?"

"Fair!" shout the first graders, including the girl on the swing.

Carlos comes by while Kim is timing the first graders. He watches for a minute, then decides to go play a game of marbles with Ben.

Ben and Carlos draw a circle with chalk on the playground. They put their marbles inside the circle. Ben goes first. He shoots three of Carlos's marbles out of the circle. Now those three marbles are Ben's.

Carlos shoots next. He misses. The boys go back and forth. Each time, Ben wins three of Carlos's marbles. After his eighth turn, Ben says, "Let me see . . . three, six, nine, twelve, fifteen, eighteen, twenty-one . . . I have twenty-four of your marbles, Carlos. Do you have any more?"

"Nope," says Carlos.

"Then I think it's time to play four square," says Ben.

"Good idea!" says Carlos.

"Anybody want to play four square with us?" shouts Carlos.

Ten kids raise their hands and run over to Carlos and Ben.

"Now what?" asks Ben. "We've got too many kids. I count twelve, including us."

"No problem!" says Carlos. "We'll draw two more game squares, and we can all play at the same time. I'll get three balls. Let's play!"

Kim decides to organize a soccer game. Carlos, who had lost at four square, joins her.

"There are nineteen kids, counting us," says Kim. "When we divide into two teams, there will be one remainder."

"So, then, what do we do?" asks Carlos.

"Don't worry," says Tom. "I'll be the referee!"

After the soccer game, Kim and Carlos decide to rest a minute by the picnic table. Soon they have company.

"Hi, Emily! Hi, Anna!" says Kim. "What's up?"

"Today is Emily's birthday!" says Anna.

"My mom sent two dozen doughnuts for my birthday treat," says Emily. She holds up two bags. "We need to figure out how many doughnuts each kid in our class gets. Can you help us?"

"Well, first we need to know how many doughnuts you have," says Kim. "A dozen is twelve . . ."

1 dozen = 12
2 × 12 = 24

"So two times twelve equals twenty-four," Anna says.

"Right," says Carlos. "Now we need to know how many kids are in your class."

"There are thirty-six kids in our class," says Emily.

"But we only have twenty-four dough-nuts," says Anna.

"I have an idea," says Kim. "Let's break each doughnut in half."

Carlos and Anna take one dozen doughnuts and break them in half. Kim and Emily take the other 12 doughnuts and break them in half.

"Now we have twenty-four doughnut pieces," says Anna.

"So do we," says Emily.

Carlos counts out 36 doughnut halves and puts them in one of the bags. "This is enough for your class," he tells Emily. "And there are twelve pieces left."

"Let's each have one piece now," says Emily. All four kids take a doughnut piece and eat it. Kim puts the rest of the doughnuts in the other bag. "You can save these for later," she says.

"Time to eat!" says Emily. She calls everyone in her class over to the picnic table to share her birthday treat.

Kim and Carlos finish their doughnut halves.
"What do you want to do now?" asks Kim.
Rrring! Suddenly, the bell rings.
"Bummer!" says Carlos.
"We have to go in *already*?" asks Kim.
Ms. Jensen calls to her class. "Okay,
everybody. Recess time is over. It's math time
now!"

"Did you say math?" asks Carlos. "We're way ahead! We've added, subtracted, and divided, too!"

"That's right!" says Kim. "We've used math all recess through!"

If you had 40 dimes, 50 nickels, and 60 pennies in your pocket, what would you have?

$7.10 and really droopy pants.

Number sense is a very important part of children's mathematical learning. When children have good number sense, they draw on several approaches to calculate with numbers. They show common sense about numbers and make sound numerical judgments. They make reasonable estimates when solving problems and can spot unreasonable answers. They are confident about applying their numerical understanding and skills to new situations.

To develop children's number sense, it's helpful to link the math they're learning in school to real-world contexts. Also, it's useful for children to have many opportunities to explain how they reason and not merely give answers.

Recess Countdown supports children's number sense by presenting a variety of mathematical situations that connect to a real-world experience: recess. Those situations are represented with the correct mathematical symbolism in the story.

The activities that follow revisit and extend *Recess Countdown*. They focus on having children explain how the situations in the story relate to number sentences and how children reason to arrive at numerical solutions. For all of the activities, be sure to keep your child's focus on explaining how he or she is thinking and reasoning. Enjoy the activities with your child!

—Marilyn Burns

You'll find tips and suggestions for guiding the activities whenever you see a box like this!

Retelling the Story

When the recess bell rang, Ms. Jensen asked the students to line up. There were 11 pairs of students. How many students were there altogether?

In the kickball game, the score was 16-16 and the bases were loaded. How many players are on bases when the bases are loaded?

When Kim kicked a home run, why did her team's score go up by four points?

Two teams with 26 players on each were playing dodgeball. How many students were playing on both teams together? Explain how you figured.

After Carlos got out 19 players, how many players were left on Kim's team? Explain how you figured.

Grace, Lisa, Kate, Nina, and Kim had a jumping contest to see who could jump the most times. Check back in the story to see how many jumps each girl jumped. Can you put the five numbers in order from smallest to largest?

At the tire swing, seven first graders need to have a turn and there are only 14 minutes left in recess. Kim told them that there was time if they each took a turn for two minutes. Explain why Kim's idea makes sense.

Ben won three of Carlos's marbles in each of eight turns. How many of Carlos's marbles did Ben win? Explain how to figure this out.

Twelve kids wanted to play four square. Explain how they could all play if they divided into three groups and had three balls.

Nineteen kids wanted to play soccer and they divided into two teams. Why did one kid have to be the referee?

Emily's mom sent two dozen doughnuts to school for Emily's birthday treat. How many doughnuts are there in two dozen?

There weren't enough doughnuts for the 36 students in Emily's class, so they broke each doughnut in half. How many halves did they have from 24 doughnuts?

After each kid took half a doughnut, how many halves were left over?

What happened when recess time was over?

Lining Up

For this activity, you need a collection of at least 30 pennies, beans, or other counters.

When the 22 students got into two lines, there were 11 pairs.

$$22 \div 2 = 11$$

Take 22 counters and line them up in two lines. Check that there are 11 in each line.

If there was one more student, making 23 students altogether, there would be 11 pairs and one extra student.

$$23 \div 2 = 11 \text{ R1}$$

Take 23 counters and line them up in two lines. Check that there are 11 in each line and one counter left over.

Without counting, take another handful of counters and place them in two lines. Does every counter have a partner, or is there an extra left over? Count the number of counters and write a number sentence to show what happened.

Do this for other numbers. Each time, put them in two lines, count them, and write a math sentence.

What do you notice about the numbers that don't have extras when you put them in pairs?

Jump Rope Problems

This chart puts the number of times each girl jumped in the jump rope contest in order:

Lisa	37 jumps
Nina	39 jumps
Grace	43 jumps
Kim	51 jumps
Kate	54 jumps

How many more jumps did Kate make than Kim?

How many more jumps did Kate make than Lisa?

Carlos says that if you counted up all the jumps the five girls made, it would be more than 200. How did Carlos know this without adding the five numbers?

Carlos also says that the total number of jumps would be less than 300. Why did Carlos think this?

Do you think that the total number of jumps is more than 250 or less than 250? Can you answer this without adding the numbers?

Emily's Class

Emily's class has 36 students. If they line up in pairs, how many students will be in each line? Will there be any extra students?

What if Emily's class divided into groups of four so everyone could play four square? How many balls will they need so every group can play at the same time?

For a class project, Emily's class divided up into groups of three. How many groups were there?

Emily's class went on a field trip. Parents drove, and five children could fit in each car. How many cars did they need?

> It may help your child to have 36 counters to use to figure out the answers to these problems. Use pennies, beans, or other counters.

More Recess Problems

Recess lasts 30 minutes. If 10 first graders each want a turn on the tire swing, how long should each swing so they all have the same length turn?

Kim jumped 51 times in the jump rope contest. "Next time, I'm going to jump twice as many jumps," Kim said. How many jumps does Kim hope to jump next time?

Ben won 24 marbles from Carlos. He had 25 marbles of his own. How many marbles did Ben have altogether?